CW01020380

PENNY&MONIQUE'S CARIBBEAN ADVENTURE

MAUREEN GORDON

ISBN: 199996750X
ISBN-13: 9781999967505
Book illustrations Shalini S

THANK YOU

Victoria, Mary Esther, Elizabeth, Joshua, Jireh, Shalom, Joanna, Leah, Pulane & Deborah for your ideas and comments during the draft of this book. And to Shalini for her wonderful illustrations in bringing all the characters of this story to life.

"This is a wonderful story with such lovely believable characters-filled with love and warmth"
Shalini S - illustrator

"Very lovely book , I was intrigued by how many different adventures they had and how they reacted to them" Eliel age 9

"I loved it, one of the best books I have read and I have read lots of books"
Joshua age 9

"The book had challenges that the children had to overcome by working together. Its funny and comical". Elisha age 12

"Well written and concise, this book gives children of other cultures a chance to learn about a different culture. It teaches about family and team work" Grace age 14

CONTENTS

Maureen Gordon

INTRODUCTION

Penny and Monique are eight-year-old twins, but not identical. Penny is the eldest by five minutes but acts years older than her sister, Monique. Penny is bossy, outgoing and adventurous; Monique is shy, likes her own company is easily frightened.

The twins live with their mother, Angela, who is a teacher and their father, Stephan, who works in a bank. Angela is taking the twins on their first Caribbean holiday to visit their Grandma Merle and many relatives in Jamaica.

The twins' experience family, fun, laughter and some scary moments on their holiday capers.

This is their story, come and join them on the adventure.

1 The Journey

Finally the summer holidays had arrived. Penny and Monique had been counting the weeks and days until the end of the school term. In two days they would be going to Jamaica and away for a whole month. They had been on holidays before, to places in the UK, and also to Spain, but they had not been away for so long before – or so far away.

The twins knew the flight to Jamaica would take nine long hours; they wondered how they would survive on a plane for so long without wanting to stop and get off. This trip had been planned and talked about and now the time had finally arrived. The girls could not contain their excitement, as on the last day of term they hurriedly said goodbye to their friends and teachers before heading out of the school gate.

Mum was waiting in the car. "Are you ready, girls?" she said.

They knew she was not talking about the car journey home, but their holiday.

"Yes," they excitedly replied together.

"I can't wait," said Penny clapping her hands loudly and laughing.

The girls began to sing, "Oh, we're going to Jamaica, back to the palm trees..." (An old song they had heard about another Caribbean country and adapted for the occasion.)

***

Most of the next day was spent packing and getting last minute items, such as sweets and snacks for themselves. Mum warned them they might not like some of the Jamaican food, but she hoped they would try it and not embarrass her.

Penny and Monique had observed their mother shopping and putting clothes and shoes away for many months. When the girls asked why she was buying so many things, she would say, "These are for your cousins and your Great Uncles and Aunt," and she would carry on with the names of more people, too numerous to remember. There were packs of English tea: PG Tips and Typhoo and Tetleys – these were a special request from Grandma Merle.

The girls wondered how Grandma Merle drank so much tea when it was so hot in Jamaica.

Once the suitcases were all packed, Penny said, "Mum, are you sure all the suitcases are going to fit into the taxi?"

Mum said, "Don't worry, girls, they will," as she sat on one of the cases forcing the zip to close whilst crossing her fingers with a smile on her face.

On the night before they flew, the girls were so excited they found it difficult to fall asleep. They chatted about all the fun things they were going to do, the people they were looking forward to meeting and seeing, especially their Grandma Merle.

At midnight Mum came into their room. "Come on, girls, you need to go to sleep now or you'll be too tired in the morning."

Penny said, "Don't worry, Mum, we will be up in time." Mum gave her a funny smile. "OK, young lady, we'll see."

***

The next morning Penny and Monique were up bright and early; they did not need to be woken up by their parents. They helped themselves to breakfast and were dressed an hour before they were due to leave.

Mum and Dad were surprised and impressed at the same time because Penny and Monique often needed an alarm clock and several calls on school days and even at weekends before they would get up. Today was different.

The girls both spoke at once to their mother.

"Isn't the taxi here yet?" asked Penny.

Monique asked, "Can we go now?"

"OK," said Mum. "Let's get the suitcases outside. The taxi should be here in a few minutes."

Dad came out to say goodbye and gave Penny and Monique his usual speech, "Now, girls, be nice to each other, don't fight and look after your mum."

"Yes, Dad, we will," they said in answer to all three requests. The girls laughed out loud and gave him a big hug. "I am going to miss you, girls," Dad said, "but I'll see you in a few weeks."

The girls' suspicions were right about the suitcase; it was a squeeze to get all of them into the taxi. They both giggled as they saw the frustration on the taxi driver's face and the mumbling under his breath. They could not hear his words, but they knew it was not pleasant.

The Flight

The nine-hour flight passed quickly for Penny and Monique as they played games, watched numerous films, got up and stretched their legs, slept, and then slept some more.

When the plane hit turbulence and the sign lit up to fasten their seat belts, the girls held hands. The excitement of the trip helped them to overcome some of the anxiety they felt. The plane went up and down and shuddered a few times before it settled. Penny felt nauseous and knew she wanted to be sick.

Mum reached into the pouch in front of her seat and gave her a brown paper bag.

Penny looked at her surprised. "What's this?" she asked.

"It's for you, if you're going to be sick," said Mum. "Be sick in here." Penny gave her mum a weak smile.

"Thanks," she said and promptly threw up violently into the bag. Monique kept her eyes closed tight and held onto her sister.

Mum took the bag from Penny whilst trying to reassure them that everything would be fine, but the girls could see on her face that she looked scared.

The captain finally announced they were over the worst of the turbulence and now beginning their descent.

Everyone began to clap when the plane finally landed. The girls had never seen this before. Mum explained that everyone was happy they had arrived safely and this was special because she had only observed this on flights to Jamaica.

The girls thought this was pretty cool, so they clapped too. They were happy to be on the ground at last. The girls felt the warm air blowing around them as they stepped from the plane. "Wow, that breeze feels nice," said Monique.

"That's the welcome breeze you're feeling," said Mum. "It's saying 'welcome to Jamaica'."

By contrast, the inside of the airport terminal felt cool. It was much smaller than the airport in London, but it was just as busy with hordes of people everywhere. The girls felt as though they were standing in line for hours whilst the customs people asked about items in their suitcases and then requested to search the largest one that contained all the gifts. The girls wondered if anything would be taken from them and kept asking their mother. Finally, they were cleared by customs and free to go.

Once outside, Angela began waving frantically at people who came hurrying to greet them. The girls were hugged and kissed by strange people all speaking at once with accents they could not quite understand.

There was Grandma Merle with Uncle Leslie and Auntie Bee (Grandma Merle's younger brother and his wife), and Cousin Thomas who was a distant relative.

Grandma Merle was crying and saying, "Look at you girls, how you've grown. I have missed you so much," and she hugged them some more. Grandma Merle looked the same as the girls remembered from seven years ago. She was a tall but stout woman with long black hair with grey streaks, which she always tied up in a bun.

The girls remembered that she used to let them play with her hair and create different styles when she visited them in England. She had a smile that lit up her face and an infectious laugh.

"Hello, Mum," said Angela.

Grandma cried again and hugged her tight. Penny and Monique felt immediately at home with the welcome they received.

"Come on," said Grandma Merle, "let's go now, I'm

sure you're all tired from your journey."

The girls were glad to get into the minivan; it was still hot outside and they felt very tired. They drifted off to sleep hearing the sounds of the different conversations of their relatives asking their mother all about life and the weather back in England.

The next thing they heard was Mum saying, "Penny, Monique, we're here now, wake up." The girls stretched sleepily and opened their eyes. At last they were at their grandma's house. The first sound they could hear was the sound of dogs barking very loudly.

Penny said excitedly, "Mum, does Grandma have dogs?" "Yes, she does. She has three, but they're more like guard dogs than pets," she said.

"You won't find them in the house, and you need to be careful around them".

" I am sure Grandma will tell you all about them in the morning."

Penny felt sad because she loved dogs. She had asked her parents for a dog many times, but each time the answer was no. They would say the flat was too small for a pet, or that the girls were too young and that a dog was a lot of responsibility, or wait until you are a little older. Penny thought so many excuses, and it seemed that she would not get the chance to play with Grandma's dogs either.

2. The Big House On Merry Crescent

P enny and Monique's eyes opened wide as they stepped out of the van and stood in front of their grandma's house. It was off the main road on a cul-de-sac called Merry Crescent. Mum had told them about Grandma Merle's house and they had seen pictures, but they never imagined it was so big.

The girls hoped to have their own rooms and secretly wished Grandma had a pool in the backyard. The house was very hot even though several fans were whirring in different corners of the large front room. Curled up fast asleep on one of the sofas was a little girl who looked the same age as Penny and Monique.

Grandma called to her, "Joanne, wake up. Come and meet your cousins."

Joanne opened her eyes and stared at the girls. She seemed quite shy but got up quickly and gave Penny and Monique a quick hug, and then disappeared into one of the bedrooms without saying a word.

"Poor thing," said Grandma. "She's been waiting up to meet you. Don't worry, she isn't shy – she's excited to meet you both. Tomorrow she will be asking you lots of questions and taking you everywhere."

"Grandma, is this really all your house?" Penny plucked up the courage to ask.

"Yes, it is," Grandma Merle said with a smile. "It's all mine. Come, I'll take you girls on a grand tour."

The house had six bedrooms each with an en- suite bathroom. Not every room was occupied, but they all had furniture and many ornaments everywhere. What Penny noticed first were three multicoloured fish of different sizes made out of glass, they were on a huge antique coffee table in the centre of the living room. There were also ceramic dogs and cats along with vases of different colours, shapes and sizes on sideboards and cupboards in all the rooms.

"Grandma Merle, how comes you have so many ornaments in your house?" asked Penny.

Grandma said, "Some of these ornaments are older than your mother, Penny."

Mum gave Penny a stern look. "Don't touch anything," she whispered, "Grandma will be upset."

Grandma Merle overheard and laughed. "Don't worry, Penny, I am sure you will be careful."

Penny felt a bit nervous after this, and throughout the holiday she tried to stay away from Grandma's prized possessions. But there were some near misses as she, Monique and Joanne would sometimes play hide-and-seek throughout the house. At times they would knock against a vase or two, each time just catching it before it would fall.

Penny and Monique kept saying, "Wow!" and "It's amazing, Grandma!" very loudly as she showed them the various rooms.

When they were shown their room with two massive beds, they screamed with delight before saying, "Thank you, Grandma, our own big bed!"

Everyone laughed. Penny and Monique could not wait to sink into them and under the clean white sheets for their first night in Jamaica.

***

Penny was up first the next morning. She shook her sister Monique whilst pleading, "Wake up, wake up, let's go and see Grandma's garden. I want to see the pool. "The girls had no idea the house had numerous grills and there were locks and bolts on every door leading to the outside – it was difficult to get out.

Grandma was already up preparing breakfast; it was only six thirty in the morning.

"Isn't it too early for breakfast, Grandma Merle?" asked Penny.

"No dear, not in this house."

"Grandma," said the girls, "can we go outside now? We want to see the swimming pool."

"The swimming pool?" Grandma laughed. "Go, but you won't find a pool." Grandma Merle jangled the numerous keys from her apron pocket and began opening the locks.

The girls looked at each other in amazement. "So many locks!" they mouthed.

They discovered there was no pool but lots of fruit trees and flowers instead, and there was so much space to play and hide. The girls were a little disappointed about the swimming pool, but they were happy that Grandma had a summer house and they imagined the many hours of fun playing in there and around the vast garden.

The girls discovered the dogs tied up at the side of the house. They barked and snarled as the girls came near.

"Grandma!" they cried and ran back into the house.

Grandma said, "You met my babies Bruno, Jess and Pele. Don't worry, they won't bite you, they're just not used to you yet."

The dogs were big. The girls were not so sure about the "not biting" part.

"After breakfast I will introduce you properly, you can help me to feed them."

After a few days the dogs seemed to have got used to the girls and welcomed them with a friendly bark instead of a growl. They even allowed the girls to pet them.

When they were not chained up, they followed the girls around the garden and sometimes into the house like puppies. This made Grandma mad, she would tell them off and say, "Bruno, Jess, and Pele outside now!" in a very stern voice. "What kind of guard dogs are you?"

The girls would giggle. At least they had dogs to play with for a while and this made them very happy, especially Penny.

3. The Old Lady Who Talked to Goats (and Other Animals)

Penny and Monique's cousin Joanne, the granddaughter of Uncle Leslie, was ten years old. When she was told that the girls were coming for the summer, she phoned Grandma Merle and told her she would be moving into her house for the holidays and had already picked her bedroom. Joanne's parents agreed immediately; secretly they were happy she was going to spend time away.

Joanne was an only child and it was hard to keep her entertained during the holidays; she was always bored and getting up to mischief. Grandma Merle was right, Joanne was not shy. When she talked it was fast and she would laugh as if telling a joke. She would entertain the girls with her many stories about Jamaican customs, school days and her friends. Penny and Monique found it hard to understand everything she said, but they liked her at once.

Grandma Merle was always saying, "Joanne, slow down, girl, they can't understand you."

Joanne seemed to know everyone on Merry Crescent when she took Penny and Monique for a walk later that day. She was calling out, "Good morning, Mr. Doug. Good Morning, Miss Julie." She would say, "Fine morning, isn't it?" in a very grown-up, high-pitched voice.

Penny and Monique laughed out loud. When she came to one house, which was similar to Grandma Merle's but much smaller, she stopped and said, "You must meet Miss Francine, she is so funny – she talks to her goats."

Joanne began calling out, "Miss Francine, Miss Francine, are you in? Call your dogs." Miss Francine came out with several dogs running and panting beside her, they barked and growled when they saw the children.

"Stop your noise and go and sit down," said Miss Francine.

The dogs immediately stopped growling and sat down panting by Miss Francine's feet but still keeping a close eye on the girls.

Miss Francine looked very old. Her skin was very dark and glistened in the sun, and the children noticed that several of her teeth were missing when she smiled. She was dressed in old clothes and wore a big straw hat on her head.

"Miss Francine, I would like you to meet my cousins Penny and Monique, they are twins and have come all the way from England," said Joanne.

Miss Francine stared at Penny and Monique for a

while before saying, "Your Grandma Merle has told me all about you two, you do look alike."

Penny was quick to say, "But *I'm* the eldest."

Joanne began to explain that Miss Francine had goats and chickens and several cats. "You want to see them?"

The girls looked at Joanne surprised that she was inviting them inside a stranger's house.

Miss Francine said, "Come on in, girls, it's all right."

She led the girls round to the back of the house into the backyard, which was very big with lots of mango and banana trees like Grandma Merle's, but this looked more like a farmyard. There were chickens and hens wandering around making squawking and clucking noises and picking at the ground. There were also several cats stretching and cleaning themselves in the shade sleepily watching the children as they passed by. There were also three skinny goats tied up, two were black and one white. They looked uncomfortable tied up in the sun and were running up and down as far as the rope would allow. As they ran they were making awful sounds like distressed babies crying.

Miss Francine began to talk to the goats, "Stop your noise, can't you see we have company, why must you always embarrass me?"

The goats stopped running and crying at once and stood staring at Miss Francine.

Penny and Monique looked at each other with their mouths wide open.

She explained to the girls that a boy normally came to take the goats out to the fields but was late today. She made a sucking sound with her teeth before adding, "That boy, he is so lazy."

She then turned her attention to the cats. "Blackie, Ginger, Calypso, why are you all lying around sunning yourself? Get to work looking for them mice that were in my kitchen having a party last night." Miss Francine made a move towards them, and the cats ran fast in the direction of the house. "Ah" she said, "them lazy cats."

Miss Francine only seemed to have sympathy for the dogs. She said in a soft voice, "Are you hungry, my babies? Your dinner is on the fire."

The dogs panted and wagged their tails and gave a soft woof. Miss Francine laughed. The girls were still watching Miss Francine closely when she said, "Come, girls, I have a surprise for you."

She led them to a wooden shed towards the end of the garden. On the floor of the shed wrapped in an old blanket were five puppies, three were black and two brown.

"These beautiful pups belong to Precious," said Miss Francine.

Precious wandered over to where Miss Francine was standing when she mentioned her name.

Penny and Monique were so excited. They thought the puppies were adorable; the sweetest cutest things they had ever seen.

"Miss Francine, can we hold them, please?" The girls pleaded.

"Yes," she said, "but you have to be careful, they are still very young."

Penny and Monique thought Christmas had arrived early for them – they were being allowed to play with puppies! Penny and Monique could not wait to tell Mum and Grandma Merle about Miss Francine and her animals.

Grandma Merle told the girls that Miss Francine was well-known in the neighbourhood and the stories about her relationship with all her animals were legendary.

"They are like her children, she has no one else," Grandma Merle said. "All her children are grown and live abroad, they don't come to visit her often. She is pretty lonely."

***

On days when Penny and Monique were not going out they would spend hours at Miss Francine's house playing with the puppies and listeninq to her talking with her animals, which Penny and Monique always found amusing.

The girls found that Miss Francine enjoyed their company. She always had snacks and treats waiting for them when they visited. The girls decided that Miss Francine was one of the nicest old ladies they had ever met.

4. First Nights: The Mosquito Trial

Penny could hear a strange buzzing sound near her ears, which she kept trying to brush away. She was half asleep and did not want to wake up, but the buzzing sound kept coming back. *Mosquitoes*, she thought and woke up properly.

Penny put on the light and pointed. "Monique look at your face," she said.

Monique slowly opened her eyes and sat up in bed.

Penny repeated, "Monique, go and look at your face in the mirror. Monique quickly ran to the mirror and screamed when she saw her face. She had several welts that had appeared which were also on her arms. They began to burn; she felt as if she was on fire.

Penny and Monique ran out of their room to find their mother. "Mum," they said, "can we stay with you? Mosquitoes are in our room!"

Mum laughed. "Girls, they're in my room, too. You can't escape them."

"What can we do, then?" they both said together.

"Whilst we are in Jamaica we need to protect ourselves," said Mum.

"How?" asked the girls, almost in despair.

"The best we can," said Mum.

Mum took ointment from her first aid bag and began to put it on the girl's spots, which brought some relief.

That night they slept with their mum and buried their heads under the sheet whilst the mosquitoes buzzed around their ears.

***

Straight after Penny and Monique woke up the next morning they ran to the mirror to inspect their bodies. Not only where the welts bigger, they found even more bites.

"Mum," they cried, "look at us, we're covered!"

It was true, the mosquitoes were everywhere and the girls could not escape them. Wherever they went in the house, it was even worse outside when they sat on the veranda.

Penny and Monique felt they were at war and sprayed the house. Mum burnt mosquito coils and candles to repel them and other bugs, but still they came.

Mum and Grandma became like nurses attending to the various lumps and bumps that came up over their bodies.

When family members saw them with the spots all

over their legs, they would joke that it was the English blood the mosquitoes liked.

Penny and Monique were not amused.

Monique had more bites than Penny because she had sensitive skin which bruised easily. She confided in her sister one day that she was feeling miserable and her wish to return to the UK just to get away from the mosquitoes.

Penny laughed and said, "Don't be silly, Monique, we have the sun, the beach, lots of space to play and its fun being here."

"I know it's fun and I love it here. I am enjoying myself, it's just these mosquitoes, they're trying to eat me alive," said Monique.

Penny thought this was funny. "Eat you alive," she repeated and collapsed into fits of laughter. As she said this another mosquito landed on Monique's bare leg ready to draw blood, but this time Monique was quick to squish it before it could inflict more pain.

Both girls laughed out loud. They began to compete with each other to see how many mosquitoes they could squish.

The mosquitoes were still all around, but the girls decided this was not going to spoil their fun or their holiday.

5. The Crab, the Suitcase and the Broom

One evening Penny and Monique were watching TV. Penny had become hooked on a quiz programme with different primary school teams competing against each other. Penny was good at general knowledge and she loved reading, so she wanted to see if she could answer the questions. The children on the programme were very quick and answered some very tricky science and math questions, which left Penny scratching her head bemused. Monique did not attempt to answer anything because she was not interested in the show, so she doodled in her drawing book instead.

Mum had gone to bed early with a headache. She complained of being worn out by the heat.

Grandma Merle was also in her bedroom lying down. The girls promised they would not be making any noise to disturb them.

"Can you hear that?" asked Monique.

Penny said, "Hear what?"

"Turn the TV off," said Monique.

As the girls listened, a scratching sound was heard coming from one of the bedrooms. It seemed to be getting louder.

"What can that be now?" asked Monique, a worried expression came over her face.

"It sounds like more of our furry friends," said Penny.

Earlier the girls had been playing a game when they watched in disbelief as a mouse had pushed its way into the lounge under a gap in the front door leading from the veranda. Although the door was firmly locked, it ran in with lightning speed and hid behind the sofa. It began to move from under one piece of furniture to another around the room. The girls had their legs up on the chair and let out a small scream every time the mouse moved. Penny thought of getting the broom, but then changed her mind as she felt the mouse was moving too fast and she might smash some of Grandma's fish ornaments instead.

The sound coming from the bedroom brought the idea of the broom back to her mind, so she went to get it from the kitchen.

Monique ran to get a small suitcase that had been left in the hallway, but she was not sure what she was going to do with it. Maybe she could get the vermin inside and take it outside to let it go, or she would use it to send it to another world.

Penny held up the broom ready to inflict harm on the creature, or creatures, as Monique slowly opened the bedroom door. Both girls gasped at the same time and said out loud, "It's a crab!"

The crab was quite large with brown markings on its

shell. The girls were not sure at first if what they were seeing was real. How could a crab have got into the house? How long had it been there?

The crab was slowly walking sideways on the outside of an airing cupboard and scratching the door vigorously with its claws. The girls were not sure if it was trying to get in or had just got out of the cupboard.

Just then, Grandma Merle came out of her bedroom. Her eyes were red and she looked upset at being woken up. "What's all this noise you girls are making?" she asked.

"It's a crab," said Penny and Monique pointing to the cupboard door.

Grandma looked puzzled. "A crab?" She saw the broom in Penny's hand and said, "Penny, give me the broom, let me kill it."

"Don't kill it, Grandma," said Penny.

Monique joined in with her sister, pleading this time,

"Grandma, please don't kill it."

"How are you going to get it outside, then?" asked Grandma.

"We'll use the suitcase and the broom," the girls said together.

Grandma Merle took the broom from Penny. "Move out of the way." She hit the crab and it fell to the floor. She gave the crab one whack and another, and then another until one of its claws came off completely. A black liquid began to ooze out from under its shell onto the floor. Monique plucked up the courage to say, "Please stop, Grandma. It's dead now."

Grandma finally put the broom down and sat on the edge of a sofa. She looked worn out and said something about her heart beating very fast. Mum heard the commotion and came hurrying out of her room. "What's all the noise?" she said looking at her mother.

"It's your children," said Grandma Merle. "They nearly gave me a heart attack with this crab."

Mum could see pieces of crab in the hallway and the broom still in Grandma's hand. She smiled, took the broom from Grandma and said, "I'm sure I will find out the story in the morning. Come on, girls, let's get what's left of this crab outside and go to bed. I think you've had enough excitement for one night."

With all the commotion, Penny and Monique had forgotten to tell their mum and Grandma about the mouse that was still running around the living room.

The crab became the highlight of their conversation as the girls got ready for bed. They giggled remembering Grandma's fight with the crab.

"That was so funny," said Penny.

"But the poor crab," added Monique.

***

Penny and Monique went to the local beach with their cousins the next day. It took them about ten minutes to walk there. They thought how brave the crab had been; to walk all that way and then find its way into Grandma's house. That was its biggest mistake.

How he got into the bedroom and into the cupboard was still a mystery to be solved.

6. The Food Adventures

Mum had warned the girls there would not be any fast food restaurants where they were staying. Penny and Monique wondered how they would survive for a month without their weekly treats.

Each time a family member or a friend of their grandmother would visit, they would bring many fruits and vegetables for the girls and their mother to try. Penny and Monique were excited to taste some of the unusual looking fruits like soursop and jackfruit. They were not sure, however, that they could eat everything people brought before they went back to England.

The girls were introduced to new foods it seemed almost every day. One of the special treats they enjoyed was going shopping in the town and being treated to a Jamaican meat patty, which was big and flat and not like the one's Mum bought at the supermarket in England. They asked for one every time they went out or if someone was going into town.

Grandma Merle introduced them to Ackee and Saltfish, the national dish of Jamaica, but too salty they thought and the ackee tasted like scrambled eggs. Uncle Leslie had picked some from Grandma's big tree in her garden, and they had them for breakfast. The girls thought it strange that ackee was a fruit but eaten as a vegetable. Penny liked it and thought she could get used to the taste. She would ask her mum to cook it when they got home. But Monique was not too sure about the taste and tried it for her grandma's sake.

One day Joanne brought Guinep, this was a small round fruit with a green shell, inside the fruit was fleshy and pink with a big seed. The girls liked them because they were sweet and tangy at the same time. Joanne could eat a whole bunch without being sick, but Penny and Monique had stomach ache after just a few each time they tried it. Mum would laugh as she also had the same problem. But they were hooked and could not stop eating them.

Uncle Leslie also came with two big green vegetables; to the girls they looked like giant footballs. Uncle Leslie said that they were called breadfruit. The girls were curious about these vegetables.

"Breadfruit?" they said together.

"Do you want to see how it's cooked?"

The girls watched as he started to gather firewood and place them on something that looked like a barbecue but smaller. He lit the wood until the fire burnt bright. The breadfruit outer skin started to turn black, first the bottom, then the side and then the top. It took some time to cook, but when it was done Uncle

Leslie put it aside and said that the breadfruit needed to cool before it could be peeled and eaten.

Penny and Monique could not wait to try it. The girls watched their grandma peel off the outer black and burnt skin to reveal the soft, yellowish inside of the breadfruit. Grandma cut it into slices and told them she was going to fry it so the outside of the fruit became crisp but it would remain soft on the inside.

The girls found the breadfruit tasted like soft white bread, but it did not have a lot of flavour. They would eat a little each time Grandma cooked it, and this was quite often it seemed to them. Grandma would say, "You girls really like breadfruit. "Angela laughed each time she saw the girls eating something new. "I am so proud of you. No more fast food for you when we get home, you will eating breadfruit from now on," she would say with a big smile on her face.

7. The Fall

M um came into the bedroom to wake the girls when her alarm went off. "Time to get up now, it's five thirty."

Penny and Monique jumped out of bed and began singing in unison, "We are going to Dunn's River, we are going to Dunn's River," whilst making up dance moves they had seen on Jamaican TV jerking their bottoms.

Mum was quick to reprimand them. "Now, girls," she said, "not those moves. Hurry up, get ready."

Penny and Monique had been looking forward to this trip ever since their mum told them about the falls back in England. They looked it up on the internet and dreamt of climbing the famous waterfall and swimming in the sea. Now the day had arrived. The sun was fully up and it was getting hotter as the girls, their mum, Grandma Merle, Uncle Leslie and cousin Joanne boarded the minivan.

After nearly three hours of travelling, along some very bumpy roads and just stopping to use the bathroom and stretch their legs, the girls were getting restless.

"Are we there yet? Uncle Leslie, are we there?" asked Penny.

Uncle Leslie said with a smile, "Don't worry, we'll be there soon. I've taken you girls along the scenic route so you can see the beauty of the island and do some aerobics exercise at the same time." Uncle Leslie was referring to the movement of the van on the road when it hit a pothole – everyone was shaken up.

Penny and Monique liked Uncle Leslie a lot. He was always making jokes and had a big, deep booming voice, which seemed to echo when he spoke. He laughed loudly at his own jokes. But Penny and Monique groaned at this attempt because today Uncle Leslie was not funny; they were tired, getting hungrier by the minute and just wanted to be there already.

After what seemed like forever to the girls they finally arrived at the falls. As they got down from the van and made their way towards the entrance, the scenery was breathtaking and the roar of the waterfall could be heard all around them.

"Wow, it's amazing!" said Penny.

"Cool," said Monique.

All the adults laughed.

The girls began jumping excitedly.

"Can we go now?" asked Penny.

"Look, we have our costumes on," added Monique.

"We have to pay first," answered Mum.

They looked at the queues – they were very long.

"Don't worry, it won't take long," assured Mum.

It did.

Grandma Merle said she had gone numerous times before and was now too old to climb the falls.

Penny, Monique, Uncle Leslie, Joanne and Mum joined a throng of people that the girls noticed were from all over the world on their ascent up the falls. They made a human chain as they climbed. Everyone was in a happy mood, laughing and joking.

Penny, Monique and Joanne were slipping and sliding on the rocks.

They could hear Mum above the roar of the waterfall shouting, "Hold on tight, girls!"

Penny lost her grip and fell into the water and stubbed her toes on a rock. It hurt and she screamed out. Uncle Leslie quickly grabbed her before she fell down any further.

"I'm fine, Uncle Leslie," said Penny, but her toes

were throbbing and her feet were beginning to ache. Penny added, "I'm going to the top."

"Brave girl, go for it," said Uncle Leslie.

Monique and Joanne also fell into the deep pools, and other holiday makers helped them up, but they were not hurt.

When they finally got to the top, the girls wanted to do it all again.

Mum said, "Penny, you can't, your toes look swollen."

"I am fine, Mum," said Penny, trying to hide her tears.

"I can see you're not fine. But if you want to go again, go."

Uncle Leslie accompanied the girls down and back up the falls a second time. This time Penny, Monique and Joanne did not slip and slide as they did the first time.

When they got to the top, Penny said to Monique, "This is so cool."

Monique nodded her head in agreement. She laughed and gave her sister and Joanne a hug.

"We did it!" they all said together.

On the way home Penny's toes were still throbbing. She confided to her mum about the pain she was feeling.

"I know you were trying to be brave, you did well today and I am very proud of you. You conquered the falls," said their delighted mum.

8. Furry Friends Re-united

Penny and Monique could be heard screaming at the back of the house in the direction of the kitchen. They were thirsty and getting some water when they saw what was scampering over the countertop.

"Mum, Grandma, come quickly!" screamed Penny.

"What is it now?" Grandma cried. "You girls are afraid of everything!"

"But it's huge," said Monique.

"What's huge?" asked Grandma.

"We think it's a rat," said Monique.

"A rat!" Grandma shouted. "There are no rats in this house!"

Monique pointed to the cooker. "It ran underneath there."

Grandma's face looked stern; it was the same expression she had when she killed the crab.

The girls ran to their mum. She led them back to their bedroom and tucked them into bed. "Don't worry," she tried to reassure them. "Grandma will take care of it."

They were not so convinced. First the mice, now rats. Monique said, "Are you sure it won't come into our room and bite our toes whilst we are sleeping."

"No, don't be silly," said Mum. "Grandma will take care of it, you'll see."

"Mum, please leave the light on," said Penny, "I feel frightened." Monique just nodded her head in agreement.

Mum kissed them goodnight and left the room. The girls had an unsettled night. Monique dreamt she was being chased by giant rats around Grandma's big house, and the rats finally catching up with her and biting her toes. She woke in a cold sweat and crawled into Penny's bed. Both girls held each other tight until the morning.

***

The next day the girls were eager to find out if Grandma had found the rat and dispatched it like she did the crab.

Grandma told them that they wouldn't find any more rats in this house again, but she would not say what she had done.

Mum told the girls that Grandma had seen the rat or rats had chewed their way into some of her favourite spices and the flour – everything had to be thrown away. That was the final straw for Grandma who did not like wasting anything.

66

Grandma was right: it seemed the rat and his family had packed their suitcases and left that night. Penny and Monique did not see or hear any more furry animals for the rest of the holiday. They were so relieved about that.

9. Waiting for Dad

Penny and Monique were looking forward to seeing their dad; they had missed him a lot. He would be coming to Jamaica for the last ten days of their holiday, and they would all return home together. They could not wait to tell him about their adventures in Jamaica so far.

Monique and Penny heard their mum say, "Your dad will be tired from his journey, so don't tell him everything at once. Give him some time to rest, please."

"Yes, Mum," they said, looking at each other and smiling.

Their father's flight was coming in during the

afternoon. Uncle Leslie and Mum were going to the airport to fetch him.

Penny and Monique were disappointed. "Please, can we come?" they pleaded.

"Not today, girls," she said. "You will see your dad in no time. He's looking forward to seeing you both."

"They will be here soon," Grandma was speaking to the girls, but it was already eight o'clock and the plane landed at four.

"That's four hours ago," said Monique, "They should be here by now."

Monique and Penny were falling asleep by ten o'clock, but were trying to convince their grandma that they weren't tired. But eventually, sleep overcame them both.

"Come on, girls, get to bed now. You'll see your father in the morning and everything will be fine," said Grandma.

"OK, Grandma," they said and reluctantly went to bed.

Grandma Merle was getting worried, too, but she did not let the girls know her concern.

***

At eleven o'clock Grandma heard the van drive up to the garage. She hurriedly went out to open the gates. "What happened? What took you all so long? I have been worried sick," she said. "The children would not go to sleep."

Angela could see how anxious her mum was. "It's OK, Mum, we're here now, and we're all OK."

Grandma Merle saw Stephan looking tired and weary but with a big smile on his face. Immediately she cheered up giving him a big hug and said, "Stephan, you're looking well, I am so happy to see you."

"Hello, Merle," he said, "do you have any of your

delicious soup? I am starving!"

It was Uncle Leslie who told the story of the heavy rainfall and the floods on the road. As they drove back from the airport, they became stuck in a very long traffic jam. Impatient drivers tried to move in front of their van and made the situation worse. People were blowing their horns and getting very upset. Angela had wished that the van had wings to fly over the traffic, but there was nothing they could do but sit and wait until the traffic moved – five hours later.

***

"Daddy, Daddy," Penny and Monique shrieked as they ran into their parents' room at eight o'clock the next morning, "we have so much to tell you!"

Dad just managed to say, "Hello," before both girls jumped on him.

10. Close Encounter Of The Cow Kind

Penny and Monique's mum and dad had been gone for two days already, the girls missed their parents and longed for their return. They had discussed back in England that they would spend some time away together when Dad arrived, which would give the girls the opportunity to bond more with their grandmother and other relatives. The girls thought this was a very good idea at the time because Mum and Dad did not get to spend much time together back in England.

The girls loved spending time with their grandma, but she always seemed so busy in the house cooking and cleaning and washing. The girls were amazed that she had so much energy when it was so hot. Grandma also enjoyed her afternoon naps and did not like to be disturbed.

"Monique, do you want to go for a walk?" asked Penny.

"I don't think we should go. Grandma said not to go far from the house," Monique answered.

"I'm bored and am so hot just sitting here, I need some fresh air," replied Penny. "Come on, we won't go far." She pointed to a path across from the house. "We can just walk down there, and then turn back."

"OK," said Monique. "Let's go quickly and come back before Grandma wakes up and notices we've gone."

The girls started walking and became deep in conversation for a while. The path led out to a vast field with trees and wild flowers everywhere, and different coloured butterflies flew from one flower to the next. Penny and Monique became fascinated as they had not seen butterflies with such array of colours before. They began chasing them hoping to catch one.

Suddenly they heard a strange noise. They ignored it at first, but it became louder and louder.

They froze with fright and slowly looked up to see three big cows with long horns and flaring nostrils blocking their path. Beyond the cows they could see a man signalling with his hands, but they could not understand what it meant. Was it for them to stand still or to run? The man was shouting at them, but they could not understand what he was saying.

Monique and Penny had never seen cows in the flesh before. One of the cows seemed particularly angry and mooed louder stamping his hooves and moving his big head around. His horns looked very pointed and sharp. Monique imagined him saying, "You better go back, you can't pass here."

"What should we do?" Monique whispered.

"Run," said Penny.

Monique said, "No, I'm afraid they'll chase us!"

"No, cows can't outrun us, let's go now," said Penny.

As Penny said, "Now," Monique was off; she did not look back for her sister. She ran so fast if it was the 100-metre dash she would have broken the world record.

Penny was not far behind. When both girls saw the house in the distance, they fell on their knees and belly laughed.

"That was close," Penny said breathlessly. "I won't be going back there again."

When they got to the veranda they laughed again. Penny said, "Monique, you left me behind. I have never seen you run so fast."

Grandma Merle was just coming out to sit down and heard the giggles. "What are you girls up to?"

"Nothing," they said, "we're just enjoying the view." Penny and Monique looked at each other and winked.

Later that evening a man came to talk to Grandma on the veranda. Penny overheard him talking about children in a field playing with cows.

"Playing with cows," said Grandma sounding shocked. "That's very dangerous."

Penny did not wait to hear any more and went to her room. She was afraid Grandma would come indoors and start asking her awkward questions. However, Penny was relieved when Grandma Merle did not mention anything the next day.

The girls saw many more cows after this on their journey around the island, but they were at a distance grazing in fields. They smiled each time they remembered the close encounter. It was to be their little secret.

JAMAICAN PATOIS FROM JOANNE

A weh you a go: where are you going

com ya : come here

A fi me: that's mine

Lef me: leave me alone

Wah gwan: what's up?

Walk good: take care

Cu yah: Look here

How yu: how are you

Meh a go deh: I am going there

Fi what: what for

To catch a fresh: To have a bath/shower

Tanks: Thanks

Maddah: Mother

Faddah: Father

11. FAMILY

Penny and Monique spent many evenings on the veranda enjoying the cool breeze and listening to the different sounds of the insects and animals noises filling the night sky. The crickets were the loudest melody makers.

The sisters loved to listen to the various stories of the family members. For example, how Uncle Marlon went to America by himself and became a millionaire. He was highly thought of in the family because he had not forgotten his roots and helped many people in the community. There was a big picture of him hanging pride of place in Grandma's house.

Another was how Uncle Leslie and Auntie Bee had also lived in England but only stayed for five years. Uncle Leslie blamed the snow, frost and fog for his troubles there. He and Auntie Bee saved as much as they could to return to Jamaica and this is where they stayed, never to venture back.

Some of Grandma's friends came and shared scary stories about Jamaican folklore, which sometimes kept Penny and Monique awake at night, but they were fascinated by them and always wanted to hear more.

Everyone was introduced to the girls as either an aunt or uncle although they were friends of Grandma and not actual relatives. Penny and Monique watched as people came to the house every day; this was exciting to them because there was always a joke or a story to be told.

Grandma's friends and family would often stay for lunch and sometimes dinner.

Some mornings there were people at the house very early and they would have breakfast as well. Penny and Monique would often whisper to their mother, "Is there enough for everyone?"

"Don't worry," Mum would reply. "There will be enough, your grandma loves looking after people. She was feeding the five thousand when she lived in England as well."

Whilst getting ready for bed one night, Penny asked, "Mum, why did Grandma go and live in the UK? Jamaica is such a cool place to be," before adding, "Jamaica, no problem, Mon," trying to imitate the accent. Mum laughed. She explained that Grandma Merle and Grandpa Fred decided they needed to earn a better living for themselves and England was the place to go.

"The best thing," said Mum, was that Grandma and Grandpa were able to help their parents, brothers and sisters who were left behind by going."

Listening to her mother tell stories of her grandparents made Penny curious to find out more. Penny thought of the word sacrifice she had learnt at school, about people who had done things at great cost just to help others. She thought about her grandparents and felt the word was the right one.

The next day Penny found her grandma sitting on the veranda sipping a homemade sour sap juice. This was another fruit they were introduced to, which Penny actually liked. When it was made into a juice it tasted like a milkshake; it was thick, creamy and sweet.

"Grandma Merle," said Penny, "can you tell me about your life?"

"My life?" said Grandma looking surprised. She laughed and gave Penny a big warm hug. "Well, what would you like to know?"

"How did you and Grandpa meet? I don't really remember him very much," said Penny. Grandpa Fred had come to the UK for Christmas, when Penny was about three years old-she vaguely remembered his laughter when he lifted her into the air and how he had got down on the floor to play horses and she had ridden on his back. Once he and Grandma returned to Jamaica he became ill and died suddenly four months later.

Grandma said, "Well, I knew your grandpa when we were both young; we went to the same school and lived across the road from each other. We always knew that we would be together some day and my parents liked your grandpa. They would say, 'That young man Fred, he has his head in the right direction', meaning that he was sensible.

At eighteen we got married and lived with your grandpa's parents. Those where good days," said Grandma Merle. "I was very young, but I had to grow up fast. After two years your grandpa heard there were opportunities for work on the railways in England. He left and said he would send for me within a year, and he did." Penny was looking at Grandma intensely; she looked so happy telling her story.

Grandma suddenly got up and returned with a picture of her and Grandpa when they were reunited in England. They were holding hands looking happy and smiling into the camera. Grandma looked pretty, she was dressed in a beautiful pink dress with a white hat and white gloves and high-heeled pink shoes to match her dress. Grandpa also looked very smart and handsome in a brown pinstripe suit.

Grandma Merle went on to tell Penny about her years in England, how hard it was to get used to the very cold winters and finding somewhere decent to live. She said to Penny, "You know, I did not think I would survive the first winter I was in England, if it wasn't for your grandpa I would have come back to Jamaica. He would encourage me and say, 'Come on, Merle, just one more year,' he kept saying until, before I knew it, we were in England thirty years." Grandma laughed out loud. "I never got used to the winters, though," she added.

Penny knew that Grandma had trained as a nurse and worked in different hospitals until she retired, and that she had received an award for all her years in nursing. Penny said, "You must really miss Grandpa."

"Yes, I do," she said, "I miss him a lot." She gave a sad sigh. Penny could see a small tear at the corner of Grandma's eyes.

"I didn't mean to make you sad," she said.

"It's OK," said Grandma, "I'm glad you asked, it was good to share some of my stories again. You are a sweet child," she said giving Penny another hug. "Good memories, good memories," Grandma Merle muttered to herself as she slowly got up and walked back into the house.

12. Going Home

P enny and Monique often shared stories of the day's adventures before going to bed. They would end up in fits of giggles about the people they had met and the things they had seen and done. They would try out some of the Jamaican Patois words Joanne had taught them and Monique had written down in a book. Both girls made a vow to each other that they would use the words at home whenever they wanted to be reminded of Jamaica.

Now there were only two days left of their holiday, and they realised how much they were going to miss spending more time on the island. The night before Penny and Monique and their parents left Jamaica,

87

Grandma Merle held a party and many people came from the neighbourhood to say their goodbyes.

The girls felt very sad to be leaving behind their Grandma Merle and Uncle Leslie, Auntie Bee and Joanne, and all their cousins.

Penny said, "Mum, when will we come back? I don't want to go home yet. Can we stay another week?"

Mum laughed. "Another week, what about school?"

"Oh, school," said Penny. "But when can we come back?" Penny said again. "I want to come back next year, *please.*"

Mum tried to distract Penny by changing the subject, but she knew that Penny would continue to ask the question until she gave her a good answer. Monique was sad, too, but she was happy to be escaping those mosquitoes at last!

. The next morning Joanne cried and held Penny and Monique tight; she was going to miss her playmates, but they promised to keep in touch

Grandma Merle kept saying, "I don't know when I will see you girls again, I am going to miss you so much." Angela said, "Don't be so dramatic, Mum, we will see you soon." Grandma Merle held the girls tight and they all cried. "Grandma, can we come back next summer to see you? We will miss you so much!" said Penny.

Grandma said, "We will see, my child, we will see."

Before they knew it, it was time to put all the suitcases in the van for their journey to the airport.

Mum, trying to cheer up the girls, said, "You have lots of pictures. You can both start to write about your adventures and make a scrapbook to show all your friends."

The girls laughed knowing that some of their friends would be very jealous as they had many stories to tell. Now they could not wait to go back to school and share with friends all about their Caribbean adventure.

Maureen Gordon

Grace Richardson

×

Lightning Source UK Ltd.
Milton Keynes UK
UKHW021100161019
351707UK00006B/22/P

9 781999 967505